THE SICK LEAVE

Hardik Sharma

BlueRose ONE.com
Stories Matter
NewDelhi • London

BLUEROSE PUBLISHERS
India | U.K.

BlueRose ONE
Stories Matter
New Delhi • London

For permissions requests or inquiries regarding this publication, please contact:

BLUEROSE PUBLISHERS
www.BlueRoseONE.com
info@bluerosepublishers.com
+91 8882 898 898
+4407342408967

ISBN: 978-93-7542-524-3

Cover design: Aafiya Saifi
Typesetting: Manisha Rawat

First Edition: December 2025

Dedicated to
all those who don’t have the time to
read this…

Teardrops in your smile

The Sick Leave

I know it will not stay quiet. I have put it off once, but it will go screaming again. The alarm knows me and I know it. It feels the same every day. My eyes need sleep, but it rings again. No, not today. This needs to stop, even if for a day. I force myself out of my blanket and search for my phone. "Feeling unwell, need rest. Kind Regards." A leave for today, and this means more sleep. So, I go back inside the blanket. But these eyes betray me, there is no sleep in them. No, I cannot let this leave go waste. I need sleep. Sleep that hours of code on black screens have pilfered away from my eyes. But it seems like sleep does not want to obey my wish. And I keep up inside the blanket, as if to snatch the warmth of a few more minutes. Something is calling me to stay in the bed, and let the time paddle by. But my mind is rushing, clocked by days of endless routine, by days of monotony. I rise up suddenly with a vague thought. I will not let this leave go away like this. Something needs to be done.

I lazily walk out of the bed and grab my bottle to quench the morning thirst. My shoulders drop, and I think. I require sleep, and I go back, with all thoughts of a few moments ago vanishing away. Many hours have passed, and I did sleep but woke up in fits of anger and anxiety. The leave cannot take away the routine. I rise up once again and clear the curtains off the windows. Bright monsoon sunlight. There is something in this bright sunlight that keeps me between the moods of deep sleep and a sad wakefulness. The balcony rails ring with sound of the newspaper being thrown across the grill. I go and pick it up. I can feel the warmth of the sun. It feels weird. Eating the breakfast slowly feels different, while my mind is rushing. I scan through the newspaper for any bits of interesting stuff. I find none. The leave is going by. I have done nothing. I am doing nothing. This would have been the hour of morning meeting at the office, but no office thought today! Suddenly an idea comes to me! I will read a novel, the one I bought a few months back and never opened.

I open the yellowish pages with feverish hands, and start reading. An hour goes by, I cannot make any sense of the story. I will continue though, for I have taken up a book after months. Hours pass by. The story is starting to open up, but my mind, alas, wanders away. I think of unfinished projects, deadlines and the meetings. No! No! Not today.

Hours pass by like this, and holding the book is now more a question of willpower. I hear droplets. A strange earthen smell rises up in my breath. I go out in the balcony. It is well past noon and the sky is full of clouds all of a sudden. It is raining softly. In a few minutes, it starts pouring buckets. I catch sight of a guard running across the society with his notebook under his arm. The rain is beautiful. Not so long back, in days of playful youth, we used to run to the roof and enjoy ourselves heartily when it would rain. Cricket with a tennis ball under rains was heavenly. The seasons are still the same. It rains almost every day in monsoons, but slowly over time we lost the music. Those closed walls hide everything. The smell of damp earth, aha, yesteryear nostalgia. I don't feel like moving from the balcony. An old tune rings up in my mind. The harmony of it and the memorable baritone. I set my chair up there in the balcony. I smile. Watercolour! I bring my old sheets back and some dry water colour cakes to paint. I set them up in the balcony. Its twilight and dark enough because of the clouds. I shift the setup inside. I am painting with eyes closed. The water flows with my colour. The book that I was reading starts making sense all of a sudden. The characters come alive. The story is good, I think. I keep on painting, thinking of the story and what it meant to say. I feel the joy rushing in my limbs. The doorbell rings. I realise that it is late evening, so it should be the maid. The day is almost over. Tomorrow everything will go back to the ugly normal of our lives. The leave is spent.

The leave felt meaningless. That which felt ill within me didn't go away. The sickness was there in front of my eyes. I keep on thinking, as if stunned by the utter reality of tomorrow. I forgot to open the door. Another bell! The meeting schedule lines up in my brain as I rise to open the door. I can sense the faint murmuring of a shiver through my spine. I see to my left. The unfinished watercolour, half wet, half dry, looks at me from the corner of the room...

The Intern

"No, this won't work! Remove the analysis, keep the simpler part, and dump that slide which shows weaknesses in the portfolio for the quarter!"

One look at her face could show that she was surprised, as well as terrified by my review of her presentation.

"Redo the entire thing and be back in an hour!" O how can I even say this to her, why am I not able to stop my lips from saying so!!

She looks dejected. She rises up very slowly, and walks slowly to the seat near the corner most cubicle. We got her here from the biggest data school in the country for two months. Bright and very smart! I would say that I was quite impressed when I saw her grip over concepts in the orientation and before, during the interviews. By evening we need to present to the management today. She has done an excellent model, very fine results, that I have just rejected. For more than two weeks she has been working hard on it, despite my repeatedly suggesting her to drop the idea. I can see her zeal for doing things, new things, innovative things, and right things. She used to stay back to discuss with others. Asked many questions. I had the same thing in me years ago when I joined the race…

Her model was indeed very good, but how to explain to her to not show all tricks up her sleeve in one go, however right that may be. The management won't get a word of it. They have hired her as an intern, not for the new work that she may deliver, but more for showing that we hire from the biggest data school in the country. I remember the day, quite early on in my career when I created that formula, and which was thrown in the bin the moment my boss saw it.

'Useless!'

Yes, 'useless' was the word he had used. He didn't even read it. That was the day I changed myself, and became a horse better fit for the race. I started doing whatever they asked me to do without question, evading any form of higher order thinking, making meaningless networks that stay only as a profile in your memory, and of which the sole utility is in getting promotions or referrals. I lost the love, and will to work. I remember how my inner self would fight with me. In moments of solitude, I would almost cry at my state. As I rose through the ranks, promotions, salary hikes, and everything, I could hear the silent sound of a deep fall within.

"Can I keep the analysis? It shows great results!" I was interrupted in my train of thought by her voice. She was standing next to me, a bit afraid of me maybe (I don't know when something that changed in me brought about a change in my appearance and way that colleagues seem to be fearful of my presence.) I try to be gentle, "My dear, in practical life, we need data and models to result in decisions. And not any decisions. We cannot go in and say that we have a statistical result that completely nullifies what was previously done by the management and rejects any further action along the same lines!"

"But doing that will deteriorate the portfolio further, as the results show. Can't we get them to know this? Maybe they will understand."

Oh, how innocent of her. "No, please, don't argue, remove it all! Quick now, half an hour left! We expect better from you!" Something choked in me as I said this. She almost ran back to the seat. I am now one of them I believe. I have lost my tongue, their words come out of my mouth, their tone, their attitude. In the starting days of my career, I would often question my bosses for rejecting my ideas without explanations. Many things cannot be explained. You get them with experience. And experience means to become like them. My mind became heavy. She came back with the presentation.

"Nice, that is the stuff we want".

A joke. In reality, the presentation was raped. It was nothing but a skeleton, that shows you nothing but only what you are ready to accept as true. I reviewed the slides a bit. One or two corrections in the language, which should always be more formal, and holding the laptop in hand, she started walking towards the room which housed the panel.

She has to present. She naturally looks nervous. I do nothing to give her any sort of confidence. She is standing right next to the screen. I sit on the corner most chair. We wait for two senior colleagues to arrive. One of them is my boss. Here he comes, hastily pushes the door, and sits just in front of the screen. "Start, be quick."

The intern is taken aback at this rush, this urgency. She fumbles a bit. "Skip the slide, next, please. Main part straight!", he says, and looks at his phone to check the time. She explains slowly, slide after slide. "Next, next, this we know, what work have you done? quick, next!"

I had prepared her in the morning for comments like these, as they are a norm rather than an exception. Just to go through the presentation, and it will be fine. She will get a pre placement offer for sure. But she looks quite nervous now. A question comes in. She answers, quite on the right track. Another question, well answered! She changes the slide, and the next slide. I am relieved, for the presentation has gone off quite well, no shouts, no insults, no conflicts.

"Our current portfolio has a very poor concentration profile and continuing with same strategy will worsen it." What! She has added the analysis, the model, the result! No, this cannot be. What she showed me was different. She added it the last minute. No! There is a moment of unnerving silence.

"What nonsense is this?" My boss turned his face towards me, I was petrified by his stern expression that had the trace of anger at the corner of his left eyebrow. "So, two months here and what you have come up with is this useless thing." The 'useless' echoed in my ears. He was speaking, or rather shouting, directly at her.

"You mean to say our entire strategy is faulty, no?" Another one came in.

"But sir, the mathematical evidence ..."

"Damn your evidence, business is not maths!"

I, who understood what she did, knew what she had done was correct. I myself had seen those patterns in the data, but years of training had taught me what not to dig. I was, somewhere on the inside, quite proud and surprised at the courage she had shown. I never had this courage in me.

"Close your presentation, what a waste!" My boss rose up and left. She was almost crying, trying to hold back her tears. Everyone had something or the other thing to say, an insult to throw at her. Can this be the moment to fight? For once in my career? I have been a dog all throughout. Can I break this? Say out aloud that she is right? I look into her eyes, which have fallen. I rise up.

"Didn't I tell you to remove the analysis! You'll never learn!" I almost shouted. The room went silent. I walked past her, pulled open the door, and went out.

That Day and the Trade

The drama of the streets is on. Buckets full of sounds and of poorly pronounced expletives are being thrown out of the remorseful windows. The fruit seller is shouting. I am inured to the nasal inflection in his rustic voice. The screen is blank! There is time still. Mumma is washing clothes. The washing machine has gone sour and the irritating gargle it produces doesn't let me concentrate. The screen, blank still. Today, I will make the trade. But for that time is there. Among all the chaos, bhajans sung by nearby aunts in the precincts of a temple can be heard. Old droopy voices that cannot hold a note properly. The rhythm covers up for their ugly voices. The screen is blank.

I have seen the screen for my life, daily, without a break, those scores of spreadsheets, thousands of codes that would make the mind numb. My ear lost the melody of the droplets of rain, and my eyes lost the warmth of sunlight. I started to prefer the dark corners of my cubicle, where, I stayed all those years. None of that stayed, except, of course the screen. That was a different time then. Second job, and a team of five. We modelled the risks that the company faced. Maybe I still remember the maths that I had to explain to my bosses with a background in sales and a high school diploma on their CVs that they had stopped updating long back. All types of risks were there, credit risk, market risk, liquidity risk, fraud risk, and even many an exotic variety of risks started coming up, like employee absenteeism risk, department dysfunctionality risk, and other names. Names, just names… When sales grew, the risk people grew, when sales fell, the risk people grew even more. The screen and meetings, and meetings that happened through the screen. Urgent meetings. Critical discussions. I remember my phone, which, on vibration caused shivers down my spine when it rang. The beloved deadline followed us like a shadow. Everything was important. We were learning a lot, ahead of our peers in the industry. Maths, codes, and data. We came up with a divine number for everything. We were the best at everything, a college tag that was envied by all, school grades to down the greatest, and the best company in the city. We were learning crazy stuff. And…

Ugh! That lame dog is barking again, someone give him something to eat. I listen to his barks. I analyse the periodic highs and lows of his barks as they faint away slowly, turning to grudges. Some time to go, today, I will make it, the trade will work, the model is ready, the results have been back tested properly, and the prediction is there, there is no scope for error. There cannot be. I slide back in my chair.

Something changed somewhere, at some time, and we couldn't sense it. The degree lost weight, and the college tag has faded. The meetings are gone. Ages go by and no call comes. Nothing is urgent anymore. Everything has lost importance. And what of the learning? That learning has left hand at the turn of the twilight of days. That learning was never there I realise. I cannot earn a penny of it by myself. No value. The maths is there, but we don't trust it anymore. One day and I lost the lovely job. Something changed. Friends are gone, some, have gone too far away. I was no better than any of them, I now understand. The gargling machine has stopped. I used to earn quite a lot in those days, but saved little. Anyways that couldn't have helped today.

I need the trade today. I have borrowed the money. I will exit the trade at noon, the model predicts it, and the risk is managed. The error distribution is controllable. The screen ticks and I enter. The street has gone silent. The fruit seller has been chased away by corrupt policemen. The old chest is right across the screen, and my high school medals and trophies, wrapped in a thick layer of dust, are looking curiously at me. High school is now a dream, a memory. I remember the girl next class that I liked. Never talked to her. Never had the courage. Spent my days and nights studying. Books, papers, mock tests, and more books. I don't know where she is now. The trophies seem to smile at me. The sunlight is changing direction, the room is becoming gloomy and dark, but the trade is going well. Thirty-five years have gone by the time I first saw this sunlight. My parents have stopped thinking about my marriage. I wanted it some time back, but now I cannot want it. So, I have made peace with the thought that I don't want it. Something has changed deep inside. The old books, the things I used to read, look meaningless now. The lectures on habits and morals have left the life of memory. A gap, a void has come in. The trade is good, I must say better. I don't want to feel happy, but cannot stop it. The days will change, they have to. The model will work. The bookshelf needs to be dusted. Time is still there for an exit.

I pick up an old favourite of mine. Thick brown hardcover, poetry, and how naïve of me to believe it all in those days. I read one stanza, dust it, and keep it back. The clock is slowly, silently, ticking away. I keep looking at it. The chair hurts my back, but I keep looking at the clock. Time is moving away and coming back. There is a pain. An old cat has been caught stealing milk from a container left unguarded. He winks at me, purrs, and goes away lazily. The clock ticks, and ticks, and ticks. The trade has started losing itself. I don't know, but I smile. The time is near. I smile even more. The old cat returns, and he also, I believe, smiles. The clock ticks. I exit. The trade is gone!

My eyes have gone dry, but my lips hold the shadow of the smile. The model was wrong. Everything is lost. The books look normal, the trophies look normal, and for the trade, I have got blood. My shoulders droop, and I let myself loose on the chair that hurts. My head drops back. I see from the corner of my eyes that mumma has lit a diya in the temple at home, and she has started her prayer. Her lips are trembling with the faint words of the prayer, and her folded hands have gone old with wrinkles.

The Upskilling Test

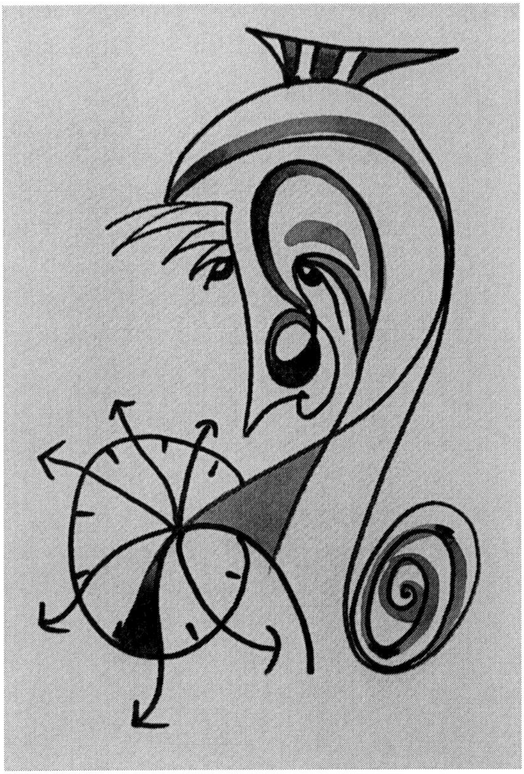

My son was in seventh standard then…no..maybe eighth, yes eighth standard only. He did not go to play cricket with his friends that day. I didn't let him go. His uniform was soiled, but I didn't care. I didn't bother to let him take it off and change. He was standing just across me. He was quiet. Only his fingers were moving, maybe due to the exhaustion of having written a mathematics exam, but I didn't worry a bit about it. My only worry was a 78 on 100 that he got in his last maths exam. The son of a topper, a topper who had won Olympiads time and again in his day, for whom maths was a given 95+ and that too without tuitions, gets a 78! Unbelievable! I didn't attend the last parent-teacher meet due to shame; my wife had to go. His soiled shirt irritated me.

"Give me the question paper!" I spurted out! He was silent, his eyes looking down. His silence frustrated me further. My wife came in, but quickly receded her steps back a bit, and stood at the entrance of the room. She had a plate with some food and a glassful of water in her hands. I stopped her. I grab the bag lying on the floor and pull out whatever I found inside. Two notebooks, one pencil, one uncapped pen, and finally, the question paper. I take out the crumpled paper, and unfold it, pressing it on all sides to remove all the creases. The first question, a simple algebra problem. Why do they need to even teach all this! But this son of mine would have got even this wrong. I take the paper, grab a pen, and thrust it in my son's little thin fingers. "Solve it". He looks up for the first time. His lips are dry. His eyes have no expression, nothing. "Do it, what you have done today in the exam". His eyes are fixed at me. I can sense fear. He writes nothing. "Write!" and I violently slap his arm. He fumbles with the pen a bit, and writes the equation in the question on the paper. He waits. "I want the answer, not the question!" He writes it, first expansion, his ugly handwriting, the second expansion of terms on the left-hand side of the equation…" Wrong!" I got up and went out of the room. I could hear my kid crying…

Today, this moment, I can see like times have played a revenge on me. My son is silent, my wife behind me is sad. I have the screen in front of me. I failed the previous upskilling test. Last chance today, else I lose my job. Those Olympiads meant nothing, and the topper is nowhere now. My son has most likely forgotten about the day when he was in eighth standard, but I cannot. The last question comes up on the screen. The new intelligence is not mathematics, and I lost all my powers in the job. I simply could not get what this new thing is. It was not logic. No one was patient enough to explain to me, like I was at one point of time. My son and wife have shown enough patience though. My wife has a tear in her eye. She's been crying since yesterday. In order that I don't see her like this, she gets herself busy all day in housework. But I know. The last question. I want to look back, but I cannot gather the nerve to see my son in the eye. "Attempts finished" A red signal beeps across the screen. My shoulders drop. My son is crying. I get up and leave the room.

The Dating App

That diary is still with me. In the corner of that old cupboard where other hands don't reach. That second half of twelfth standard. Her class was just beside the staffroom. She was beautiful. The curl at the upper parting of her hair would often come off the forehead towards her eyebrow and would roll across her ear in a curled fashion. Her smile had this tomboyish jump that thrilled me. I knew her since childhood, and all through the years, the soul, the genius in me grew with her. When my hands wrote the first poem for her, then the second, then the third, and the diary grew thick with the weight of my heart. I was never myself who wrote that, but some genius made me write it. She might have known my love for her somewhere, but I never told her. She had someone else. But the songs would never stop on the diary. Every word was divine, every stroke of the brush was coloured by the genius that love gives you. I picked up the harmonica, and don't know how learned it in a week, as if some divine inspiration from some earlier birth attuned my ears to the heavenly notes. I could see music in me flowing at all hours. Reason could never go where the genius went. Oh, how beautiful she was. The divine genius stayed with me, even after the day I saw her last outside the examination centre, and even after the day I threw the diary in the corner of the cupboard that no one opens. Leaving her grew the passion at first, the words became heavy with some unknown meaning, and the canvas turned more obscure. Random people would ask me its meanings, and I would have nothing to say. I would hide myself and the genius behind the veil of ignorance. I could not forget her, but, time flew, and slowly, very slowly, I saw the genius going away. Days would go by and I would have nothing to draw, no lyric to write. All poem seemed nothing but a forced rhyme, a forced philosophy, and the brush lost the touch of the soul. Years have gone by…

I have progressed in life, moved on as they say, with a good job, good money, and luxury to spend it all on. The diary never came out. The canvasses stay rolled in some other forgotten corner. Many a female friend I met through all these years, but the genius, the mad divine genius never showed up. I would avoid conversations for I would have nothing to say. But I would intently listen. Relationships, what she needs, what you need, responsibilities, pasts of one-another, future you want, long-term or casual, dating apps, money, trends and everything. But no word was spoken about the genius. A genius that didn't require a checklist for love. These conversations would turn up to me often, to be turned back, as

I would have nothing to say, just a frown to revert back. Often the conversation was made to jeer at me, and then turned back. I wasn't the only one single in these conversations, but others had a marked presence in attempts on dating apps which were meant to create matches and where you could find partners. I was nowhere. I was often labelled from an 'ascetic' to a 'closeted romantic', and someone in a fit would throw up a 'virgin' towards me. I could do up with all this, but matters became worse as the years went by.

Family started pressing me for marriage, and I had no idea with whom. At lone moments, it felt like cheating the divine genius. Career progressed even further, money came in my accounts and the corpus grew, and somewhere I was coming to terms with the fact that I had lost the genius forever. My friends never believed in the genius thing. They told me it was my talent that did all of it. A friend, in moments of wisdom, advised me to leave it as a teenager's madness. But the genius was the reflection of love. I used to remember those last moments when I saw her in front of the examination hall, quite back in the day. I had no fear, no grief. I was happy, and watching her with another did never make me jealous or fearful. That genius was mad, and was strong, and flew like a free bird across the horizons of soul. Now I could sense a fear within myself. Family calls were mounting up and I was spending hours in frustration. I stopped going to the conversations. I would spend hours strolling beside the river, staring blank at the old buildings and silent chimneys. I was losing hope, and out of sudden fit, I downloaded the dating app that everyone talks about for a match. I slowly created my profile. I spent days scrolling by, and a bitterness swelled in me. It wasn't very different than getting a job with a fabricated CV, since the profile could speak nothing of me. It was words and numbers. I kept on scrolling, without any attempt for a match, without any interest.

And one day, scrolling out of a routine, I was shocked. I could feel my heart beat in my head. She was there. The curl at the parting had stayed. With trembling fingers, I zoomed the profile pic. The eyes were the same, and the lips still had that tomboyish jump, albeit a bit lesser. My fingers were trembling, I felt numb. My lips prayed for the divine, but no song was coming to me. No music, no design flowed through me. I kept looking at her pic for many an hour. It was very still, silent, she looked the same, everything was there but something had changed. I don't know. I could feel my eyes coming heavy with tears that were hard to hold back. With trembling fingers, I swiped left and uninstalled the app.

The Interview

I feared this would happen one day. The unemployed who came for their dosage of intoxication at my cigarette shop told me about it. It has happened with others. Now it's my turn to go through this. What an ugly face he has! His dark eyes look straight at me from across the table. The eyes are unmoving, stern, and the purpose is clear. But the wrinkle at the corner of his cheek shows a futile poignancy. The intelligence meter is right at the center of the table, between us both. The room is very dimly lit. He still looks at me, making me naturally avoid his eye. I was preparing my betel leaves when the goons came to pick me up (kidnap me rather) and put me in this room. My hands are tied, and I haven't had my dose today, which is causing me irritation in the spine. He looks at me. The expression is unmoving on his face. Yes, this is the dreaded interview.

I am not the first one to go through this. It all started a few years ago. The unemployed told me. These unemployed, who were then bosses in companies like these, created this weird intelligence. They were toppers from different schools. They had brains. Mathematical principles and scientific approaches were there in their back pockets. They were the fathers and mothers to this intelligence. But like the outstanding nepo kid, the child outdid the parent. Whatever they did, the intelligence started doing better. They studied hard, the intelligence studied harder, and in half the time. They thought logically, the intelligence learned it better, and very soon, pointed out the flaws in their creator's thinking. They worked long hours, but the intelligence could work round the clock without rest. Whatever new they could imagine was already given by the intelligence. Research institutes closed down. Education became meaningless. And suddenly, the topper was gone. No one could then understand, let alone accept what was happening. The creed of the analyst and engineer vanished. Company bosses were out, unemployed. Only the top folks stayed, who went street after street, looking for people who defied what the intelligence did, who could think beyond the logic of the intelligence. History professors were kidnapped. Artists were taken away. And now, small vendors like me are being taken for the interview. As far as the legality of the whole thing mattered, they could shut it up with money.

"Tell me one most important factor for running a successful business."

Hein, did he just ask a question? Has it started, the first interview of my life? "My dear, tell me the one most important factor for running a successful business!"

My head was blank. Had I thought of all this during my school days, I wouldn't have ended up at the cigarette shop that my father runs. Can I call it successful? Maybe. What is the factor then? He wants one. Nothing is coming in my mind, oh no, I cannot think anything! Never thought about all this. The meter has turned green! Why? There is a smile on the person's face, which came for a moment or so and then receded into the same old expressionless expression. Maybe this means that the intelligence couldn't predict my response as there was no response at all. So maybe, it cannot predict nothing! Phew! A tough one. Me, who found the simplest of sums tough to solve during schooltime, these people would obviously be mad to expect me solving these complicated questions.

"Lovely my boy!" he says. The smile comes and recedes again. My hands are tied and it irritates me. "Hey, get this rope off my hands!", I yell out of frustration. His eyes grow big, and he ignores my plea, which fires us the irritation further.

"Tell me some of your weaknesses"

"You ****, untie the rope and then I will tell you all about my weaknesses. I will break your teeth, you ****"

The meter turns green, instantaneously, and the person gets up from his seat, with that same smile, that stays a bit longer, as if he cannot control his happiness, but he sits again and tries to be normal. This meter I see is mad. You call this intelligence? This intelligence that can take nothing apart from reason. This intelligence that cannot entertain doubt. How can this intelligence take away jobs of these smart people? One unemployed, a regular customer, mentioned it to me once. It's not as if the unemployed haven't sat through all these interviews feigning irrationality, but years of scientific training has imbued their irrationality even with so much of logic and reason that they fail to fool the intelligence. Courses and medical schools have come up to cure this disease of excess rationality. I really pity this intelligence and its creators.

"Now my boy, one final question, and we are done!"

I am least interested. My shop is open, the thieves wouldn't wait. Everyone steals these days. "Leave me you ****, I have a shop to run, don't have time for this buffoonery, business, weakness, asshole!" He smiles again. "This is exactly what I want boy. History teachers don't have it. Impatience! Intelligence has all the patience in the world, we no longer need it from mortals".

"Leave me, you fool, who made you the boss here!"

"Amazing, amazing, I absolutely love it!"

I tried to control myself, knowing that this oldie has lost it completely. "Okay, ask the last one, quick!"

"What do you think the intelligence does not know?"

"Addition and subtraction, okay, now you see I am not fit for the role, let me go!"

The meter turns green, the person jumps, comes across the table to hug me. He starts crying. I was utterly confused. "This what you call intelligence cannot add?" His eyes were moist. His voice choked. "No, my boy, it very surely can, however it never expected someone like you to think that it cannot!" And he hugged me again. He went behind the chair to untie the rope. "You've got the job my boy" and hugged me again. "Our first employee in years!"

I carefully open the folded offer letter in my hands.

I drop it on the sideways while going out.

The Loneliness of a Friday

I fear the weekend. Fridays are spent in the office room thinking of what to do in next two days. The office room where we all are existing, without the other knowing, in the lone company of work and laptop, of calls and deadlines. But at least the time doesn't feel heavy on the heart. Today is a Friday. The question of how to get over the coming two days is lingering in my head for the last hour. The mail for an early release has come, which has added a few hours of worry to the routine.

The new management trainee in the risk team has already left. Something over time has made me dull enough, such that I don't have any confidence of talking to any one, letting alone the idea of asking her for a few hours of company on a Friday evening.

As I logout and walk out towards the metro, I think of the not so old days, when I was full of passion for everything. We were in college. I was no stranger to music and fun, and we would wait for a Friday evening to come with its joy. It seemed as if anything could give us pleasure. For some time after that, I found joy in the memory of those days, but it faded with time. Everyone got busy, got a career to look after. Everything has come to random messages once in a quarter or more, and just that. At some time, I have told myself the blunt lie that I am progressing in life. Let's now leave this story.

The metro is full of faces. A person standing next to the door looks relieved. The girl standing just next to me is expressionless, soaked deep in the incessant scrolling of the social media app on her phone. She receives a call from someone, and affirms her presence with a very soft 'Yes' that drops from her lips. A small boy brushes across my knees with her mother chasing her all about in the coach. The question of what to do stays. Should I go for a movie? No, no. There is no fun watching movies after movies when you cannot discuss them with anyone. It's not that I have no one to talk to, family, a few friends, but the longueur of days that needs company has never been there, in this big city. In some random moment of thought, I have often texted an old friend or so, with detached conversations coming to grey ticks and messages not seen for days. I don't blame them, it's all right. Oh, I realize I have missed my station. Well good it is, the longer I stay away from my dimly lit flat, the better. But the return trip was quick and I need to get off.

I pet the lazy cat that sleeps outside my flat at odd hours, and enter the dimwit room. Three books and a notebook on my bed. Have been trying to get the flair back for a few months now, but has not led anywhere. Anyways, I think I will watch some new web series. Binge watching is the way to budge through time that this Friday gives you. Something long, that can keep you hooked for days. I keep scrolling on the screen. I cannot fix up my mind on one thing. Frustration. I get up the old novel I was trying to read and read a few pages at length. Time passes. I take up my phone out of a habit and open the social app. Stories everywhere of Friday night fun. Or maybe I see that everywhere and ignore the rest. Confirmation Bias. I uninstall the app and throw the phone on the corner of the bed in frustration. I had placed my finger at the point where I left reading, so I read again. I read about backyard cricket. I strikes me suddenly out of nowhere that it has been years since I have last rolled my arm on a cricket field. There were days when you could go to any park in the neighbourhood, and ask yourself into any random group playing. Do my fingers still remember the carrom ball that I perfected on the streets? Or that back of the hand slower ball that would come with a loop and drift sometimes towards the batsman? My fingers need the ball. I hurriedly rush to open the cupboard and scramble under the pile of unwashed clothes to look for the ball that I kept there a few months back. I planned to join the academy, even did so, but found out in a short span that I was quite out of age in the midst of teenagers trying to build a career out of the game. Street cricket, and even park cricket has been lost to the city. Yes, found it! The feel of the seam sends a thrill down my spine. Until the realisation that I had no one to play with. I threw a few carroms on the wall, some backspin would drift that in before straightening up. And I left the ball and started looking for some web series again. I pick up my phone, her number turns up. We talked on text a few days back. An old college friend, didn't chat for years. But it was a nice thing, she was very welcoming. I called her. The sound of a familiar voice, when it gets to you after ages, and that too on such a Friday, can lift your spirits up my miles. We had nothing to discuss apart from some old days. Eight minutes, but a day. I don't know what happened. I took the ball in my hand and got downstairs to the court where no one was there. That run up of 2.5 steps, that uncanny action, that flick of the finger and the back spinning carrom with a beautiful follow-up. I could imagine the ball taking the outside edge as the invisible batsman misses the line because of the inward drift. Or a leg before. The ball makes a dud sound as it hits the wall. It rolls back slowly towards me. I find company in its soft rolling towards me. I walk slowly and pick up the ball. I smile. I am alone here. Wow! What a Friday!

The Investments

The tea has gone cold. The biscuits are moist due to the excessive humidity. The feeling of family breakfasts is gone. As I lay my back against the old sofa, I hear a soft monotonous dripping of water from the tap. This dripping goes on and on, the whole day, the whole week, and for months it stays so. Every drop needs to be stored. The supply of water will now be in drops, the municipality announced. We need to collect as many that can be collected in a day, and see what can be done. A cup of tea needs to be planned in advance of a week. Bathing is illegal. The only running supply of water is for the hospitals and army.

"Hey, did you check how much we have?" My father asks me.

No, he is not talking about water. He is talking about gold. Retirement planning has gone haywire. As if when throats went dry, people realised that this shiny metal is of no use. When the useful went scarce, the useless lost value. I remember in my undergrad economics course, we were taught the diamond water paradox. Well, there was no paradox. Gold and diamond are all garbage now. Dustbins across the streets are full of it. I heard of attempts by the municipality to convert gold to food and water. The search of an alchemist for thousand years has been reversed.

"A few kilos left" These few kilos were nothing but a liability now. All useless assets have seen their heyday. Mutual funds have tanked, banks have gone bust, insurance companies are history, as without the useful, the useless doesn't return value. No one would survive to see the day when they generate return, so the day comes closer and closer, and bust! I have seen my wallet filled with notes going empty in half an hour, as no one accepts these. Everyone wants something of value against something of value. What is value?

I am thinking a lot. I should walk a bit. The street is bare. The afternoon hour. Street corners have been taken up by the homeless ones, the ones who saw the fall of destiny before us. Unemployment is a thing of past now. Gone are the days when universities would commission economists to write mathematical papers on why all this happened. Long time that we realised as a race that the why does not matter, for what is happening cannot be changed by explanation.

The sun is still bright. Years of human misery hasn't dulled the sun a bit. It is still shining as it used to do before, in the good times, or say, different times. A man is coming across the road. Seeing me, he stops, comes closer, and hugs me. Hugs are of value. He drops a tear, and walks past me. I keep walking. I sit at the corner of the adjoining street. The sun is showing its red. A cat is teaching her kitten to jump across the building. She does so once, and meows. The kitten seems confused and afraid. She coaxes him again. It jumps, and crosses. The cat licks it in love. A smile goes through the afternoon street.

I walk back home. I have got my return on investment.

The Deadline

"Huddle, quick, room 4, now!" The message popped. I got up. A few others in the team were alarmed. We almost ran to room 4. The manager was walking nervously about the room. Before we could even enter, he blurted out," The latest figure for recovery along with the data, 3 pm, deadline! Go! Quick!" Then as we were about to turn back, we saw him shouting, "3, not a second late!"

We were all quiet and went away as quickly as we had come. 3 was impossible, everyone knew. 15 minutes left to 3.

Simply not possible. The data team will give data in 30 minutes at least. Then cleaning it. Then the figure and its calculation. I have the previous figure. Won't help. Need fresh data. The latest one. If we don't get it? What will happen? I cannot face him. No!

"What to do?" One asked. I tried to get my focus back on the present.

"How to do?" Another added.

"Tell him it is impossible!"

"Mr. Senior kindly do the favour."

The senior was helpless. He was the only one who could confront the manager on this. He walked back to room 4. He went in. We heard shouts from the glass cabin. He came back running straight to his desk and picked up the call. We all knew what this meant. Our faces dropped. My forehead was burning with sweat. I scrambled across the set up for the old data. Oh no! I have forgotten which folder I saved it in. I tried taking a few deep breaths to calm myself. I still don't seem to remember the folder. The elevated voice of the senior on call with the data team was audible to everyone. He left the call. He cried, "No chance!"

I scrambled for the folder. "Try the other drive", a colleague standing just behind me said.

"But that's the old data, we want to new one", someone said. You could sense the fear in the few voices that spoke.

The senior called, "Get some estimate of the figure, call! Ten minutes left to 3."

Oh, I found the folder, and the data! "Good", the senior said. "What's the figure?" "40" I replied.

"The estimate?" the senior shouted on the colleague who had called some other team to get the estimate. "Not yet senior, just a sec!"

Another one came in, "We can't show the estimate, he wants the actual figure. We don't have the data! We don't know where he needs to present these! If a wrong figure goes to senior management, we are all gone!"

"Even if we get the estimate, we still don't have the data. He asked for the figure and for the data!"

The senior didn't reply. "Estimate?" he shouted again. 8 minutes left.

"Just in, 55 sir".

Others were busy calling the data team, no answer.

"Data?"

"No!"

"Any chance?"

"Looks like no!"

5 minutes.

The senior walked towards me and bent a bit. He paused, as if caught somewhere, between two minds. Then he went back.

"Senior, 4 minutes."

A message from manager pops up right at the moment. "The figure, guys? Not a minute late. Don't forget the data!"

The senior receives a call, "Yes sir, just in sir, coming!"

We all scream, "We don't have it"

He comes back towards me. Gathers everyone and says, "Take the total as 55, create the entries for the data. Use some random number generator. Keep the total 55!"

He paused. "And start looking for jobs! Mail me the data in 2 minutes!"

He said this and went running to the manager, shouting out aloud 55, 55!

The Resignation

The button blinks on the screen. It has been half an hour since the last call with boss. The resignation portal is open on the screen in front of me. This is not the first day I have done this. They pay me extremely well, and I have crossed many a ladder in my job. I have enough in investments to last many a year, maybe this life. Then what to fear? The absence of a job offer in hand?

It is a Sunday today. I was playing with my kid in the backyard. He was gifted this toy gun by a relative a few days back, that makes a harsh sound when clicked. I was teaching him how to hold it properly, when I felt something vibrate, a vibration that my ears catch first of all the frequencies on earth, and I hate my ears for that. It can be anyone, but I know who it will be, at this odd hour, on a Sunday. It's strange, and very sad, but it is what it is. I reluctantly walked up to the table and picked up the call.

"Join the meet! Urgent!" He throws up straight.

"Not at home, outside, can't!" These years have taught me how to lie blatantly at any moment.

"Come back, join in 15 mins, critical, no option!" He hung up.

I frowned a bit and felt a deep pain in my nerves just above the ear. I forgot everything. My kid, his gun, my wife in the kitchen. That gun…an old picture of a smaller me holding a plastic gun at an annual event at school came to my mind. I wished to become a commando. Oh, that face of me, I remember! I realised that I was a ghost now. Light has receded from my eyes, hours of sitting in front of the screen have given me an ugliness, that shows up in the fat that I have got across my chin. I remember my father took that photo. He was cheering for me from the stands. Yes, my father. They wanted me to become a commando. I have never figured out why the parents who brought you up to be amongst the stars became smugly satisfied when their kid gets a job and a stable pay. The commando was long gone. The words of courage and dedication to the nation went away once the money came in. I don't remember when and how my marriage happened, but it was soon after getting the job. A belly has come up over the part of the skin which was once as tight as a rope, and running up a few stairs has become almost unimaginable. Army became history and a forgotten dream.

The thought quickly shifted to the meeting. What for? Why do I imagine so much? I ran my hand through the table and caught hold of the anxiety pill. No, no, she said, "No pill!". I kept it back. Then took it again and swallowed it. No water.

It has been 45 minutes in front of the resignation portal. I didn't join the meeting. Five missed calls. That vibration. Twenty messages. I didn't open a single one.

What will I do if I resign? Was it this that was stopping me from clicking on the button? If no job, then what? My child was pulling my leg for a second round of play.

My wife came from the next room. "What happened?" she asked, wiping her wet hands with a towel. Then her expression changed. "Meeting? Again? Sunday!" She stayed for a while. Then went back inside. As I said, I don't remember much of my marriage. I don't know what marriage is, even after being with her for years. I never talked to her properly, never a deep thought, no conversation. I remember the date of our anniversary, but struggle to buy a gift for her. I don't know what she likes. Never asked her. We were strangers. I don't know what she thinks of these meetings, that come up on weekends, or when I stay up late at office for work. She never complained, but her eyes have been sad always.

Again, a call, again I don't attend to it. The button blinks. "Count your blessings! People are at a worse off station in life than you." A boss once told me. A mail pops up. Another one. Again, a call.

My kid is still at my leg. I look at him. He is bigger now. Growing every week. I laugh. Blessing, oh yes it surely is! I feel my eyes widening up. I snatch the toy gun from my kind's hand and rise from the chair. I can feel the commando. The button is still blinking. I shut down the laptop and smile. And I smile again. I open the screen, click on the button, and shut it again! I go out in the backyard, almost pulling my child by hand. The toy gun clicks!

One day when it rains
I will open the window
To hear the old memory of love
And to smell the seasons gone cold
Through the bitter shiver of it all…

That day you might come
I will hold your hand
And we might go away
Leaving behind us an open window…